This book belongs to

....

Walt Disney's

Lady and the Tramp

Storybook Favourites

Reader's Digest Young Families

Walt Disney's
Lady and the Tramp

Illustrations by The Walt Disney Studios

Story adapted by Teddy Slater

Illustrations adapted by Philippe Harchy

$\mathcal{L}$ady was a lucky little cocker spaniel. She had everything a dog could want. Her beloved owners, Jim Dear and Darling, had pampered her since puppyhood. They gave her the tastiest titbits to eat and the softest bed to sleep in, and they showered her with lots of love and affection.

Lady returned this kindness by waking her master each morning with a gentle lick on the cheek. And while he was at work Lady stayed close to her mistress, protecting her from any possible harm.

But one day everything changed. As Lady told her friends, Trusty and Jock, Darling now seemed more interested in the tiny sweater she was knitting than in her faithful friend.

Lady's pals quickly put two and two together and guessed that Darling was going to have a baby.

'Babies are extremely sweet,' Trusty the bloodhound said.

'And very, very soft,' Jock the Scottie added.

'Why, a wee babe is nothin' but a bundle of –'

' – trouble!' an unfamiliar voice chimed in.

The voice belonged to a scruffy stranger named Tramp. Though Tramp had no family of his own, he seemed to know quite a lot about babies – and none of it was good.

'Take it from me, Pigeon,' Tramp told Lady. 'A human heart has only so much room for love and affection. When a baby moves in, the dog moves out!'

Although Tramp's words worried Lady, she couldn't believe her family would ever be unkind. And once the baby was born, Lady saw just how wrong Tramp had been. For not only did Lady still have her owners' love, she now had one more person to cherish and protect.

Everything was fine until Jim Dear and Darling decided to
take a short holiday.

'Don't worry, old girl,' Jim Dear told Lady before they left.
'Aunt Sarah will be staying here to care for you and the baby.'

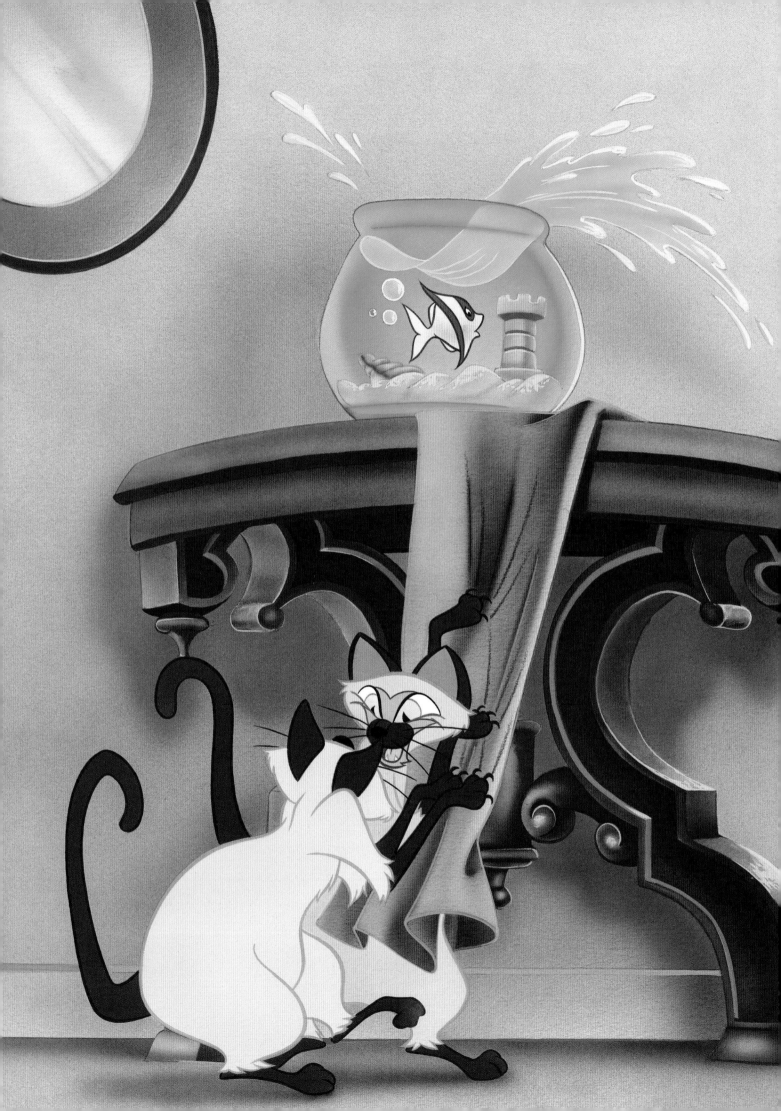

But Aunt Sarah soon made it clear that she did not like dogs at all. To make matters worse, she had brought her two nasty cats along. Lady watched helplessly as they wrecked the living room and terrorised the goldfish and the bird.

When the cats went upstairs, however, Lady sprang into action. She raced ahead to stop them from entering the nursery. The nasty creatures tried to run by her, but Lady stopped them in their tracks with a threatening growl.

Aunt Sarah heard the commotion and poked her head out of the nursery. She took one look at Lady growling and the two cats snivelling, then ran to protect her pets.

'Oh, my precious pusses,' she crooned. And scooping the cats up in her arms, she carried them gently downstairs.

Then Aunt Sarah dragged Lady off to the pet shop. 'I want a muzzle for this vicious beast,' she told the shop assistant.

'I have just the thing,' the shop assistant replied, placing one of the awful contraptions over the struggling dog's face.

In desperation, poor Lady ran out of the shop.

Outside, a pack of stray dogs began to chase her. Horns blared and tyres screeched as Lady raced blindly through the streets, across the railway line and into a strange and scary part of town.

Her heart pounding, Lady ran on with the strays yapping at her heels. Just when she felt she couldn't take another step, a brown ball of fur rushed to her side.

Biting and barking, Tramp fought off Lady's attackers until every last one had turned tail and slunk away.

Tramp helped Lady to remove the hateful muzzle, and then she told him her tale of woe.

'Poor Pidge,' he said when she had finished her story. 'You sure have had a terrible day. What you need is a night out on the town to cheer you up!'

Tramp led Lady to a quaint little Italian restaurant. There they shared a delicious plate of spaghetti and meatballs while musicians serenaded them with a romantic tune.

After dinner, Lady and Tramp took a moonlight stroll. When they came to a patch of wet cement, Tramp scratched a big heart in the middle and placed one of his paws inside it. Lady did the same.

A silvery moon was high in the sky when the two tired dogs finally snuggled up under a tree and fell fast asleep.

When they awoke the next morning, Lady was horrified to realise she had spent the whole night away from home.

'Aw, Pidge,' Tramp said, 'there's a big wide world out there just waiting for us. Why go back at all?'

'Because my People need me,' Lady replied. 'And I need them. Besides, who will protect the baby if I'm not there?'

Tramp had no answer to that. He simply bowed his head in defeat. And even though Lady was sad to leave Tramp, she could hardly wait to return to her family.

But, when Lady got home, an angry Aunt Sarah was waiting for her. 'I have a special place for you now,' Aunt Sarah snapped as she led Lady to a dog kennel in the back garden. 'This should keep you out of trouble!' she said, chaining Lady to a stake in the ground.

That night Lady was moping around the garden when a big grey rat scurried out of the woodpile, scampered up the porch railing, and darted into an open upstairs window.

'That's the baby's room!' Lady cried. She dashed forward but was jerked to a painful halt by her chain. Lady began barking frantically to attract Aunt Sarah's attention.

Aunt Sarah finally appeared at the back door, but only to yell at Lady. 'Stop that racket!' she said before slamming the door shut again.

Just then Tramp raced into the garden. He had heard Lady barking and had come to help her once more.

'There's a rat in the baby's room!' Lady said. And with no thought for his own safety, Tramp ran inside to get the rat.

Tramp reached the nursery in the nick of time. While the baby lay sleeping in the crib, the rat was ready to pounce.

Tramp struck first. Fur flew and furniture fell as dog and rat tore around the room. The rat was fast and fierce, but he was no match for Tramp.

By the time Aunt Sarah burst in, there was no sign of the rat – just Tramp and the topsy-turvy room. Aunt Sarah thought Tramp had been after the baby, and she quickly called the dogcatcher. 'Don't come back, you vicious brute,' Aunt Sarah warned as Tramp was carried off to the pound.

As soon as Lady explained what had happened, Trusty and Jock raced after Tramp. They chased the dogcatcher through the dark and stormy night.

When a taxi appeared out of the fog, the dogcatcher's horses reared up and his wagon toppled over. Jim Dear and Darling were in the taxi. They had come home and discovered the rat. It was clear then that Tramp had been protecting the baby, and they set out to find him. He was a true hero!

Jim Dear and Darling decided to take Tramp into their home.

'This is where you belong,' Jim Dear told Tramp. 'You're part of our family now.'

And soon Lady and the Tramp had a family of their own – three pretty pups, who looked just like their mother, and one mischievous Scamp, who clearly took after his father.

Walt Disney's Lady and the Tramp is a *Disney Storybook Favourites* book

Walt Disney's Lady and the Tramp, copyright © 1979, 1991, 2005 Disney Enterprises, Inc.
Story adapted by Teddy Slater. Illustrations adapted by Philippe Harchy.

This edition was adapted and published in 2009 by
The Reader's Digest Association Limited
11 Westferry Circus, Canary Wharf, London E14 4HE

Editor: Rachel Warren Chadd
Designer: Louise Turpin
Design consultant: Simon Webb

® Reader's Digest, the Pegasus logo and Reader's Digest Young Families
are registered trademarks of
The Reader's Digest Association, Inc.

We are committed both to the quality of our products
and the service we provide to our customers.
We value your comments, so please do contact us on
08705 113366 or via our website at
www.readersdigest.co.uk
If you have any comments or suggestions
about the content of our books, email us at
gbeditorial@readersdigest.co.uk

Printed in China

A Disney Enterprises/Reader's Digest Young Families Book

ISBN 978 0 276 44465 4
Book code 641-024 UP0000-1
Oracle code 504400016H.00.24